This book belongs to:

_____

For Betty and Jack, with fond memories.

Nicola and Charlotte

OXFORD
UNIVERSITY PRESS

Great Clarendon Street, Oxford OX2 6DP

Oxford University Press is a department of the University of Oxford.
It furthers the University's objective of excellence in research, scholarship,
and education by publishing worldwide in

Oxford   New York

Auckland   Cape Town   Dar es Salaam   Hong Kong   Karachi
Kuala Lumpur   Madrid   Melbourne   Mexico City   Nairobi
New Delhi   Shanghai   Taipei   Toronto

With offices in

Argentina   Austria   Brazil   Chile   Czech Republic   France   Greece
Guatemala   Hungary   Italy   Japan   Poland   Portugal   Singapore
South Korea   Switzerland   Thailand   Turkey   Ukraine   Vietnam

Oxford is a registered trade mark of Oxford University Press
in the UK and in certain other countries

British Library Cataloguing in Publication Data available

ISBN: 978-0-19-272865-4 (hardback)
ISBN: 978-0-19-272866-1 (paperback)

2 4 6 8 10 9 7 5 3 1

Printed in China

Paper used in the production of this book is a natural,
recyclable product made from wood grown in sustainable forests.
The manufacturing process conforms to the environmental
regulations of the country of origin

CHARLOTTE MIDDLETON

presents

CHRISTOPHER Nibble

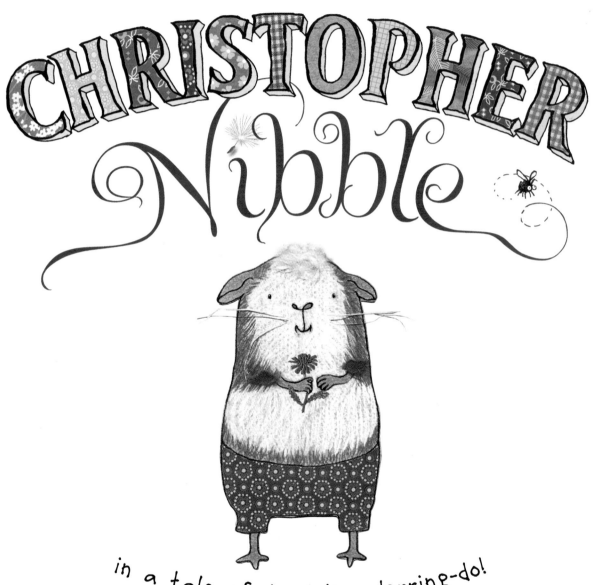

in a tale of dandelion derring-do!

OXFORD

UNIVERSITY PRESS

If there was one thing Christopher Nibble **loved** more than football,

it was . . . .

eating dandelion leaves.

He ate dandelion leaves. . .

at breakfast time,

at lunch time,

and at dinner time.

And if Christopher felt peckish between meals, he ate. . .

MORE dandelion leaves!
But it was not just Christopher who liked
dandelion leaves. Mr and Mrs Nibble liked them.
His sister liked them. His friends liked them.

In fact... every guinea pig in Dandeville **loved** dandelion leaves.

munch

munch

nibble

munch

nibble

All day long the happy sound of munching and nibbling filled the air...

until, that is,
dandelion leaves
began to
run out.

Dandelion dishes
were taken off
the menus, and
dandelion drinks
disappeared from
the shelves.

Menu Today

Carrot and lettuce wrap on
a bed of ~~dandelion~~ leaves
cabbage

~~Dandelion~~ soup
cabbage

cabbage
~~Dandelion~~ and
broccoli quiche

Dandelion
~~juice~~ sold out

The last few leaves could be bought
on the internet...

for a HUGE amount of money!

Soon the worst thing imaginable happened...

all over town the dandelions had been munched to nothing more than bitten-down stalks, and the guinea pigs had to make do...

with chewy cabbage instead!

Just one dandelion was left but nobody knew about it, except Christopher Nibble. It happened to be growing right outside his bedroom window.

Christopher's mouth
watered at the sight of it.
But he knew he mustn't eat it,
or let anyone else eat it,
not if it was the last dandelion in town.

It might even be the last dandelion
in the whole world!

He thought hard and decided. . .

... to go to
the library.

He borrowed a book called 'Everything You Need to Know about Dandelions'

and he read it very carefully.

He found a little cloche to protect his dandelion. . .

and every day he watered it and picked off the bugs.

Every day he was very
good about not taking
even the tiniest
little nibble
while he . . .

waited,

and waited,

and waited.

Until, finally, his dandelion had grown the most beautiful white head of tiny seeds.

Very gently,
Christopher picked it
and carried it all
the way up
Daisy Chain Hill.
When he reached
the top . . .

he had just
enough puff to take
a deep breath and . . .

The seeds filled the air...

and landed gently all over Dandeville.

At first nobody noticed.

But soon the new
plants started to sprout
fresh leaves.

And in no time at all Dandeville
was filled with the happy sound
of munching once more.

As for Christopher,

But now there's something he loves just as much as **eating** dandelions. . . .

Christopher loves GROWING them!